# Sophie

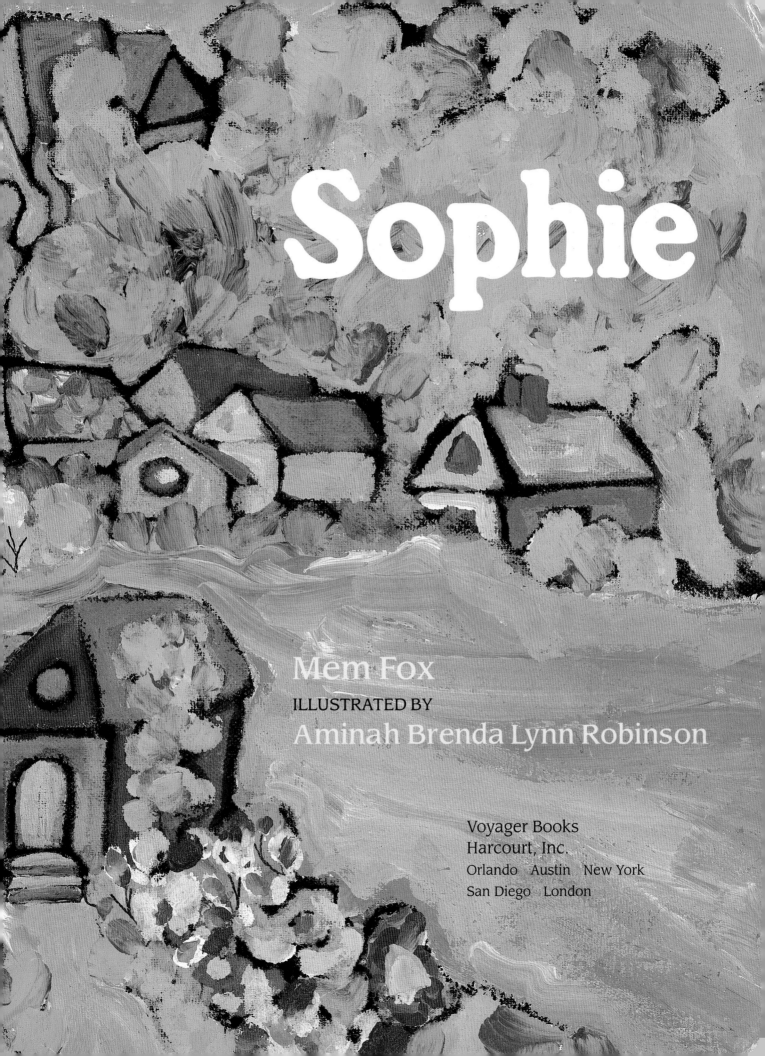

# Sophie

Mem Fox

ILLUSTRATED BY

Aminah Brenda Lynn Robinson

Voyager Books
Harcourt, Inc.
Orlando   Austin   New York
San Diego   London

First Voyager Books edition 1997
*Voyager Books* is a registered trademark of Harcourt, Inc.

Library of Congress Cataloging-in-Publication Data
Fox, Mem, 1946–
Sophie/written by Mem Fox; illustrated by
Aminah Brenda Lynn Robinson
p.    cm.
"Voyager Books."
Summary: As Sophie grows bigger and her grandfather gets smaller,
they continue to love each other very much.
ISBN 978-0-15-277160-7
ISBN 978-0-15-201598-5 pb
[1. Grandfathers—Fiction.  2. Death—Fiction.  3. Birth—Fiction.]
I. Robinson, Aminah Brenda Lynn, ill.  II. Title.
PZ7.F8373So     94-1976

TWP   T S R Q P O N M

Printed in Singapore

The paintings in this book were done in acrylics, dyes, and
house paint on rag cloth.
The display type was set in Gorilla and the text type was set in
Leawood Book by Thompson Type, San Diego, California.
Color separations by Bright Arts, Ltd., Singapore
Printed and bound by Tien Wah Press, Singapore
Production supervision by Stanley Redfern and Jane Van Gelder
Designed by Lydia D'moch

For Frank Hodge
—M. F.

In memory of my father
—A. B. L. R.

Once there was no Sophie.

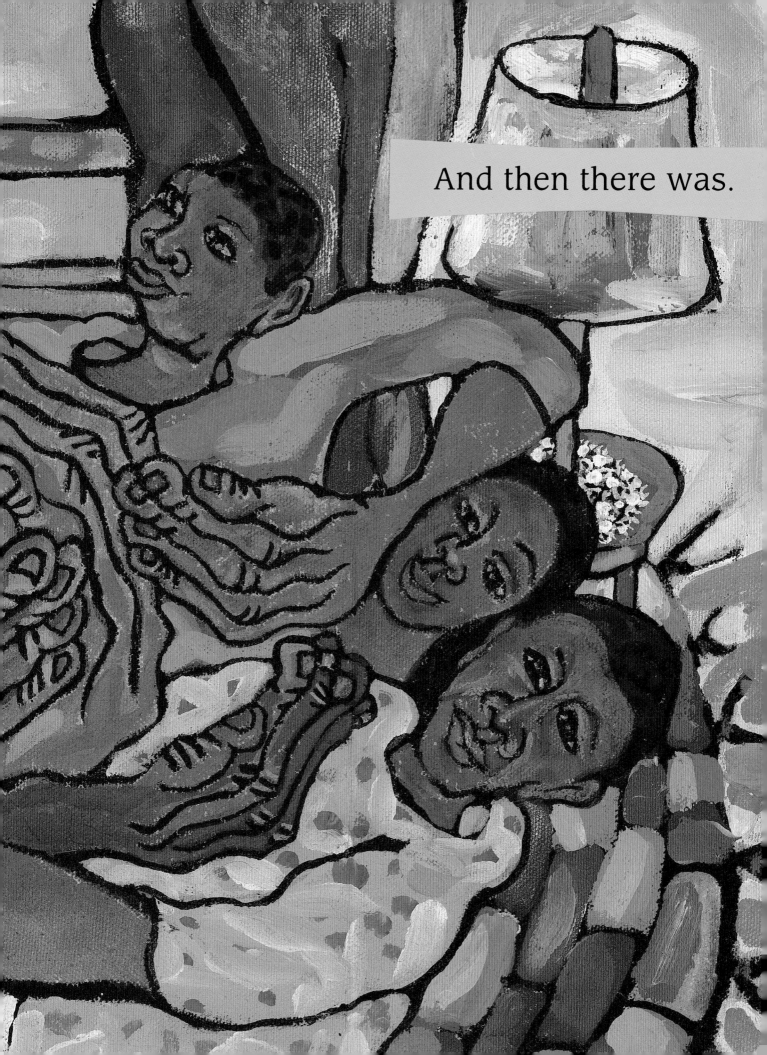

And then there was.

Sophie's hand curled
round Grandpa's finger.

Grandpa and little Sophie
loved each other.

Sophie grew

and grew

and grew

till she was big enough

to work with Grandpa,

big enough to look Grandpa in the eye.

Grandpa grew older

and slower

and smaller.

Sophie and little Grandpa loved each other.

Grandpa's hand held on to Sophie's.

And then there was no Grandpa,

just emptiness and sadness for a while,

till a tiny hand held
on to Sophie's

and sweetness filled the world, once again.